A

BOOK

Published by STORYSACK LTD
Resource House   Kay Street
BURY BL9 6BU

ISBN 0-9540498-4-5

First published in the UK 1999
Second Edition 2002

Printed in the UK
by Carlton Press Group
Units 4 to 7 Britannia Road
Sale, Cheshire
M33 2AA

If only ...

**a garden story
written by
Neil Griffiths
and illustrated by
Judith Blake**

storysack

STORYSACK LTD

One afternoon in early summer, a small black caterpillar crept nervously from beneath a stinging nettle leaf. It felt the warmth of the sun brush against its back as it peered inquisitively into the garden beyond.

Attracted by its beauty, it crawled towards a bed bursting with early summer flowers. It gazed at heavy-headed foxgloves, fragile drooping peonies and delicate pale geraniums, but it was a bright red poppy which caught its eye.

geranium

There, dozing in the very centre of the flower head, lay a plump, white tailed bumble bee, exhausted from collecting nectar.

The caterpillar admired its velvety coat of black and yellow and sighed:-

"If only I had such a splendid coat."

The bumble bee opened one eye lazily and grinned knowingly.

The caterpillar was then startled by a ray of sunlight which had caught the wings of a dragonfly hovering above a deep purple water iris.

It watched for some time as it darted in the sky above, hypnotised by its delicate beauty.

   "If only I had rainbow wings," it sighed enviously.

The dragonfly peered at the caterpillar below and chuckled knowingly.

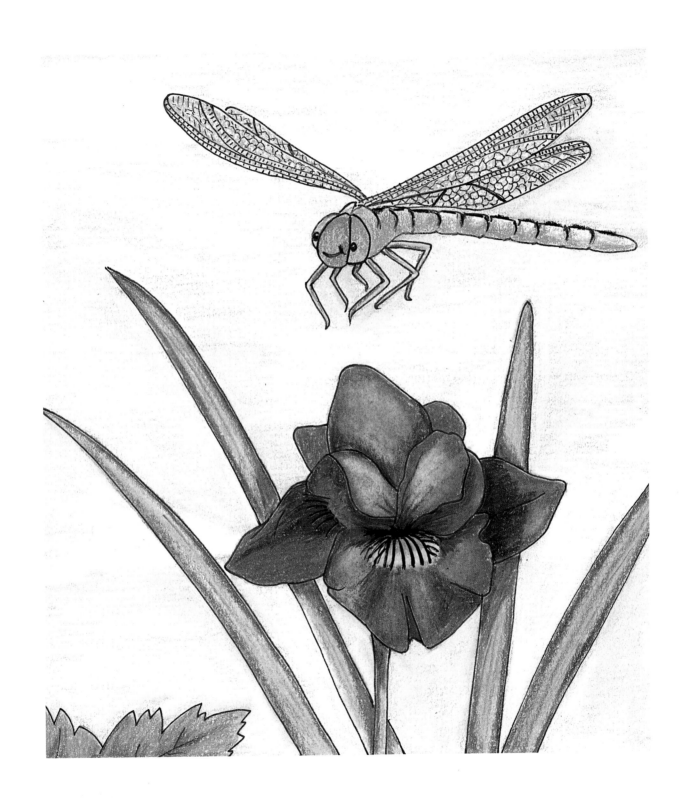

Suddenly a meadow grasshopper leapt from behind a lupin and landed by a clump of sweet smelling lavender. There it burst into song, in the hope of attracting a nearby mate.

The caterpillar listened in awe to the grasshopper's music making.

"If only I could sing such a beautiful song," it sighed.

The grasshopper paused from its singing, glanced over its shoulder and laughed knowingly.

Thinking it was being made fun of, the caterpillar decided to climb a tall sunflower stem to hide.

Higher and higher it climbed, gripping tightly with its tiny feet, until eventually it reached the top and nervously inspected the giant flower head.

It was not alone, as a two spot ladybird had flown in and was scuttling about busily in search of juicy green aphids.

The caterpillar looked on longingly and whispered,

"If only I had such a dazzling wing case of polished crimson and black."

The ladybird stared at the caterpillar and giggled knowingly before flying off in search of more green aphids.

The caterpillar felt suddenly alone and somewhat tired after its long climb.

It decided to take a short cut to the garden below along a tiny silken strand.

The strand was attached from the flower head to a flower pot, which had been left carelessly lying around by a gardener.

Lupin

Nearing the end of its descent, the caterpillar suddenly froze at the sight of a network of tiny threads.

The architect and builder of this masterpiece, a garden spider, was busily adding the final finishing touches to its day's work.

Dangling from the leaf of a delphinium, it spun furiously as the caterpillar made a hasty descent to the flower bed below.

   "If only I could weave such a fine work of art," it sighed.

The spider paused from its work and smiled knowingly.

In need of sleep, the caterpillar found the flower pot to be the perfect place for a well deserved rest.

Supported by a thread from the roof of the pot, it discarded its dull outer coat and replaced it with a new tough outer skin.

There it fell into a deep sleep full of strange dreams and sensations for sixteen days and sixteen nights.

It emerged from this deep sleep, feeling cramped and confused. For several hours it struggled to break free and feel again the warmth of the summer sun.

Eventually its efforts were rewarded as it fell to earth with a bump!

Feeling weak and crumpled, it sought the comforting warmth of the garden beyond. It breathed in the sweet scent of orange blossom, rose and honeysuckle as new life pumped through its veins.

In the flower bed beyond, tiny pairs of eyes could be seen, watching and waiting. Slowly, one by one, each pair of eyes emerged from its hiding place.

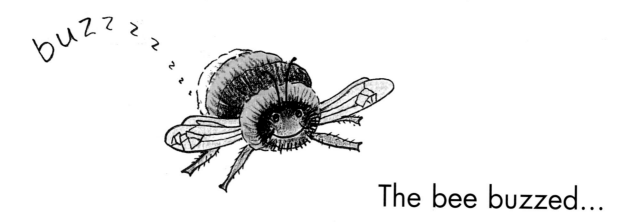

buzzzzzzz

The bee buzzed...

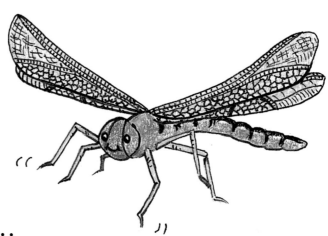

the dragonfly danced...

the grasshopper hopped...

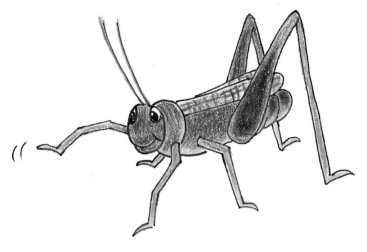

the ladybird fluttered...

and the spider spun, as
they looked on in admiration.

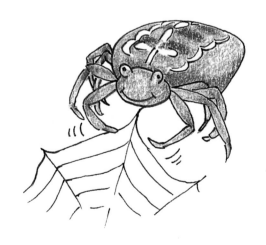

"What are you looking at?" asked the butterfly.

"You!" they replied together.

"Me?" asked the butterfly.

"Yes, you!" they replied.

"Why would anyone want to look at me?" sighed the butterfly sadly.

The garden creatures all winked knowingly.

The butterfly took a closer look at itself and could scarcely believe its eyes. It gazed in amazement at the rich symmetry of shape and colour contained in each of its fragile wings.

"You must have known!" said the butterfly excitedly.

"We knew!" replied the garden creatures.

"If only I had known too!" said the butterfly proudly.

The End